DiGBY O'DAY

Up, Up, and Away

Text copyright © 2015 by Shirley Hughes
Illustrations copyright © 2015 by Clara Vulliamy

First U.S. edition 2016

Library of Congress Catalog Card Number 2016932810
ISBN 978-0-7636-7444-1

LEO 21 20 19 18 17 16
10 9 8 7 6 5 4 3 2 1

Printed in Heshan, Guangdong, China

This book was typeset in Bodoni Antiqua.
The illustrations were done in pencil, ink, and digital collage.

Candlewick Press
99 Dover Street
Somerville, Massachusetts 02144

visit us at www.candlewick.com

Up, Up, and Away

Shirley Hughes

illustrated by

Clara Vulliamy

CANDLEWICK PRESS

for Mark, with love from Clara

for Martha, with love from Shirley

Contents

And some fun extras at the back!

Today we're talking to Digby O'Day and his friend Percy. They always manage to find adventure — wherever they are!

Hi, Digby and Percy! First of all, can you tell us something you've always longed to do?

DIGBY: *I long to have a plane of my own. I would name it after my aunt Daisy.*

PERCY: *I long to do ballroom dancing—on ice!*

Ah, so, Digby, you'd love to get up, up, and away! In that case, where are you both happiest: on land, on water, or in the air?

DIGBY: *Well, as soon as I get over my fear of heights, being in the air would be very exciting.*

PERCY: *Yes! As long as we remember to bring a picnic . . .*

If you could fly anywhere, where would you choose?

DIGBY: *I would fly somewhere with lots of long country walks.*

PERCY: *I would fly to a tropical island where I could relax under a palm tree with a fruity drink.*

Would you prefer to be able to fly or be invisible, and why?

PERCY: *If I were invisible, I could visit my friend Digby without Lou Ella looking angrily out of her window at me.*

DIGBY: *I would love my car to be able to fly—what an adventure that would be!*

And finally, tell us a time you were especially brave.

DIGBY: *I prefer to be modest about it, but I did rescue our friend Mr. Canteloe when he fell into the sea.*

PERCY: *And I stuck up for Digby in the school play. He forgot his words, so I ran onstage and joined in loudly!*

Well done, Digby and Percy — you are brave adventurers. Thank you!

Ariel
Likes:
playing the trumpet
playing chess
ice-skating

Lou Ella
Likes:
fast cars
new things
getting her own way

Lou Ella's
friends
Like:
afternoon tea

Bill the
balloon man
Likes:
balloons

The police
Like:
keeping the roads crime-free

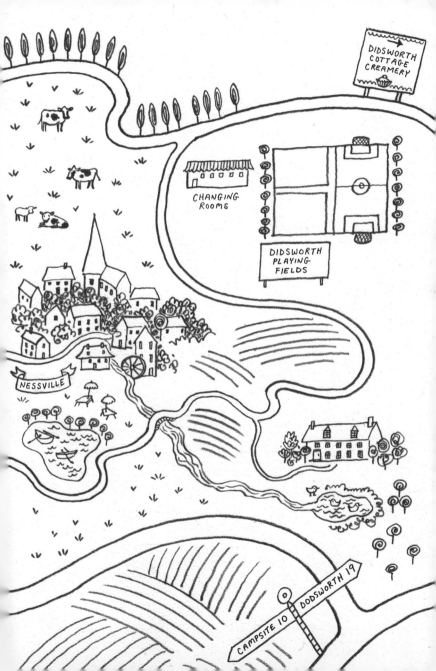

Chapter One

Digby O'Day was very proud of his car. He cleaned and polished it every weekend, and his friend Percy often came to help.

One Saturday, when they were
giving it an extra shine, Digby said,
"This is a really good car, but one
day I'd like to try a different form of
transportation."

"It still runs well," said Percy
encouragingly. But he added, "As
long as you don't try to pass in the
fast lane."

Digby's car had given him trouble
recently when, during a slow crawl
home from the shops, the engine had
failed during a traffic jam, and he and
Percy had ended up pushing it all the
way home.

Don Barrakan at the garage had repaired it in no time, of course.

But even so, there were times when Digby daydreamed about being effort-lessly airborne—up, up, and away!

6

Digby's irritating neighbor, Lou
Ella, bought an expensive new car
every year. She liked new things: new
clothes, new cars, new furniture,
and new kitchen cabinets. She even
changed her pets
quite often.

She had already tired of her goldfish because she thought he was boring . . .

and her Siamese cat because he sharpened his claws on the carpet . . .

and her hamster because he kept her awake at night running and running on his little wheel.

She had given them
all away to her friends,
one by one.

Now she had bought
a parrot, which she was
teaching to speak. His name
was Ariel.

She had spent a lot of
money on a beautiful parrot
perch, which she placed
in the bay window of her
house so that passersby
could see her interesting
new pet.

She devoted a lot of time to
grooming him, glossing up his
feathers, and manicuring his claws.
Ariel endured this in pained silence.

She even took him for rides in her car, though Ariel simply sat hunched in the seat beside her.

She was always trying to get him to talk, but Ariel refused to say a word.

Her friends called around to admire him.

"Can he talk?" they asked.

"Oh yes," Lou Ella answered, "of course he can. But he's a bit shy with company."

Privately she went on urging him
to speak . . .

but she was not
a patient lady.

"Come on, why don't you say
something? The man at the pet shop
assured me that you were a very good
talker. So why don't you say 'Pretty
Polly' or 'Who's a clever boy?' as
other parrots do?"

But Ariel remained stubbornly
silent, sitting on his perch.

One morning, when Percy was helping Digby to shore up a bit of collapsing trellis near Lou Ella's garden wall, they saw Ariel pacing restlessly back and forth.

"Good morning!" Digby called
out. To his surprise, Ariel answered:
"Good morning to you, sir!"

"I didn't know you could speak!"
said Digby in astonishment.

"Of course I can," Ariel replied. "I just don't care for Lou Ella's boring conversation. She keeps trying to make me say silly, pointless things. She doesn't seem to realize that I am a highly educated bird. It's too humiliating! My confidence is getting so low, I've almost forgotten how to fly."

After this they often chatted over the garden wall when Lou Ella was out. And they soon discovered that Ariel was indeed a very interesting bird . . .

with many hidden talents.

Chapter Two

On Saturday morning, Percy came hurrying around to Digby's house bursting with excitement and waving a leaflet.

"Look at this, Digby! It's an announcement about the big Air Show, right here in Didsworth!

DIDSWORTH AIR SHOW

displays·flights·teas

today!

It's at the playing fields today. There
are all sorts of aircraft—gliders,
helicopters, hot-air balloons! Come
on, we can't miss it!"

As they were leaving, Digby caught sight of Ariel hanging about in the garden as usual.

"Why don't you come with us?" he cried. "Quick! Before Lou Ella sees us!"

Ariel needed no encouragement.
He hopped joyfully
over the gate

and they all
set off together.

They arrived at the Air Show,
where they found a wonderful sight.
There were so many different kinds of
aircraft on display.

People were lining up for
demonstration flights. Big crowds
gasped and cheered as they took off.

One of the biggest attractions was
the hot-air balloons, now tethered
to the ground and floating gently,
looking like great colored Easter eggs.

Digby had always dreamed of learning to fly and imagined jumping into the cockpit of his own aircraft and taking off . . .

until he remembered how scared he was of heights.

The three friends wandered around, fascinated by all the exhibits. Ariel turned out to be very knowledgeable about all types of aircraft. Early flight was one of his specialities.

DiGBY O'DAY

Meanwhile, Lou Ella, back at her house, had discovered that Ariel was missing. She had searched every room and all over the garden, but he was nowhere to be found.

"That willful bird!" she muttered. "He must have gone off somewhere without asking my permission."

She went out and looked up and down the road. Then she caught sight of the leaflet that Percy had dropped, lying near Digby's front gate. She picked it up and read it.

DIDSWORTH
AIR SHOW
displays·flights·teas

toda

"So that's it!" she exclaimed. "I bet Digby and Percy have gone off to see the Air Show and have taken Ariel with them! It's just the sort of thing they'd do. Well, I'll soon fetch him back!"

She put on her special motoring hat, jumped into her car, and zoomed off.

By this time, Digby, Percy, and
Ariel had managed to edge right up
close to one of the hot-air balloons.

The friends watched the sandbags being removed and one of the men in charge adjusting the guy ropes.

They were so fascinated that they were quite unaware of Lou Ella in her car, pushing her way through the crowd, honking her horn angrily.

She was getting closer and closer
and was almost upon them
when Ariel spotted her.

"Quick! It's Lou Ella!
Don't let her catch me!"
he squawked, and
dived into the
balloon basket.

Digby and Percy
vaulted in, too, and
crouched down.

But Lou Ella had already caught sight of them! She jumped out of her car and elbowed her way through the crowd toward the balloon.

Chapter Three

Just as Lou Ella reached them, there came a sudden gust of wind. The guy ropes of the great balloon had been left untied, and it began to take off—slowly at first, then rapidly gaining height—up, up, and away!

"Now we've done it!" said Percy grimly. But Ariel was delighted. He was strutting up and down along the edge of the balloon basket, flapping his wings in triumph.

"We're off! We're off! You can't catch us now!" he squawked.

They looked down at the faces of
the crowd, quickly receding below.
There was Lou Ella, purple with rage,
shouting something that they were
already too far away to hear.

It was a beautiful day. The sky
was full of little fluffy clouds. A brisk
wind soon carried the balloon high
above the town, over the rooftops,
and out into the countryside beyond.

They had no idea where they were heading or how to steer, but for a while they were happy to just drift along.

Digby discovered that if they pulled
a certain rope, the balloon went up,
and if they pulled another, it went
down. They could not make it go
faster or slower. So for the moment,
they decided that the best way to go
was *up*.

Ariel gallivanted about, sometimes
perching on the edge of the basket,
opening his wings wide, and sometimes hanging upside down from one
of the guy ropes.

Meanwhile, Digby and Percy
leaned over the side, watching
the shadow of the balloon
tracking them below.

After a while, Percy said, "It must be nearly lunchtime. It's a pity we didn't bring a picnic!"

"What we need is an island to land on," exclaimed Ariel. "Like the one I lived on long, long ago, when I could fly, with lots of fruit and nuts and a sparkling stream of fresh water."

"Good idea!" said Digby. And he
added, "If we can find one, that is . . ."

Chapter Four

But now the weather was changing. The sun disappeared behind dark clouds, and it began to rain. It was hard to see where they were going or what was below.

Soon Digby and Percy were soaked through and shivering, but Ariel did not seem to mind being wet. He spread his wings wide, fluttered upward, and strutted up and down.

"Here we go, into the bright blue yonder! Flying high, happy and free!"

"Bother the blue yonder," muttered Digby, peering anxiously into the gray mist that was gathering below. "I think we should try to land."

His fears seemed justified when there was a sudden loud crack of thunder overhead and a flash of lightning ripped through the sky.

Now the rain came down in torrents, beating against the balloon and soaking them all.

The high winds were making the
balloon rock dangerously. Percy clung
to the side of the basket, while Ariel
hung on to the rigging with his claws.

Digby was desperately trying to
bring the balloon down, but he
couldn't see anywhere to land. At last
he saw some bright lights and—yes!—
something that looked like an island!

They began to descend and, more
by luck than good navigation, landed
right in the middle of it.

Chapter Five

Cautiously, they climbed out of the basket and looked around them. They were surrounded by dripping bushes and a few trees, but from quite nearby they could hear the steady rumbling of heavy traffic.

"I don't think this looks quite like the kind of island I was hoping for," said Ariel. "It looks more like a traffic island to me!"

He was right. Instead of being surrounded by clear blue water, all they could see was an endless stream of trucks, cars, and motorcycles roaring past. None of them stopped. They were all too intent on reaching the motorway.

"Looks as if we're stuck here for a while," said Digby.

"Oh dear!" squeaked Percy. "And it's been such a long time since breakfast!"

Their first thought was to secure the balloon to a tree, then shelter as best they could under the bushes.

The storm was now showing signs
of easing up. The lightning had
stopped, but the rain still came down
relentlessly.

They were all soaked to the skin.
Digby felt in his pockets, hoping
he might find a bar of chocolate he
had forgotten about. But there was
nothing.

"Perhaps we could rig up some
kind of shelter to keep the rain off for
a bit," he suggested as cheerfully as
he could.

They all set to work. Ariel
collected twigs and leaves, and the
other two brought fallen branches
and tried to make them stand up
like a tent.

But they were not very good at it, and despite all their efforts, it collapsed in a heap.

"I wish I'd paid more attention when we learned this kind of thing in the Didsworth Forest Folk Fellowship," said Percy.

"Though I did get commended for my egg custard," he added.

"I'm afraid that's not much help to us now," said Digby rather shortly.

They huddled together, waiting for the rain to let up and listening to the roar of the traffic.

At last they heard the sound of a car slowing down and the honking of a horn. They rushed through to the edge of the bushes.

There was a car
parked there, all right. . . .

It was Lou Ella's car! She had leaped out and was standing right beside it, arms akimbo!

Chapter Six

"Come here *at once*, Ariel!" shouted Lou Ella. "I've wasted enough time following you and your friends all over the place in that silly hot-air balloon. Now you're coming home with me, my boy!"

But now, to her astonishment, and for the first time in their relationship, Ariel spoke to her.

"No, I will not! In my view you are a highly unsuitable person to own a pet, and I have no wish to belong to you, no matter how luxurious your home is. And to tell the truth, your conversation bores me stiff!"

Lou Ella was flabbergasted!
She lunged at Ariel. He let
out a wild squawk and flew
high up into a tree.

But for Digby and Percy, there was
no such means of escape. Lou Ella
had them cornered.

At that moment, they heard the piercing wail of an approaching police car. It drew up sharply, right behind Lou Ella.

Two traffic officers got out and strolled toward her. She had quite forgotten that she had parked her car in a traffic roundabout.

Quickly, she put on a false smile and tried to apologize.

"I was just going to move it!" she cried, but it was no use. One of them was already taking out her notebook.

Digby and Percy seized their chance. They raced back to the hot-air balloon, and Digby leaped inside to prepare for liftoff. Ariel flew down and perched on the edge of the basket. But just as Percy was about to scramble aboard, there came a great gust of wind and the balloon started to take off.

"Wait for me!" shouted Percy. But it was too late. The balloon was already rising quickly into the air. Digby leaned out of the basket as far as he dared and held out his hand to Percy. Their fingers touched, but then they were pulled apart.

"Don't leave me!" cried Percy, terrified.

Ariel reacted swiftly. He picked up
a rope that was lying in the bottom
of the basket and flew down with it in
his beak. Percy caught hold of it as
Digby grasped the other end.

The basket rocked dangerously as,
just in time, Digby managed to pull
Percy inside. He landed
in a breathless heap.

Ariel flew up
after him, very pleased with himself,
squawking,
    "Did you see me *fly!*
        Talk about
            quick off the mark!"

As they rose higher and higher,
leaving the traffic island behind,
they looked down on Lou Ella, who
was being given a parking ticket
and a severe lecture
by the police.

Her motoring hat had fallen awry,
but she was still protesting shrilly:
    "It was only for a minute or two,
I tell you!"

PARKING
TICKET

OFFENSES:

OBSTRUCTION ☑

RUDE
BEHAVIOR ☑

IN BIG
TROUBLE?

YES ☑
NO ☐

Chapter Seven

It was late afternoon by now. The
rain had cleared at last.

"Time we were getting home," said
Digby. "If the wind will blow us in the
right direction,
that is."

Luckily it did. But as they drew near to familiar landmarks, Ariel's mood changed and he became very quiet, sitting on the side of the basket.

Digby and Percy noticed that a
great many birds had now begun
to gather and were flying alongside
them, keeping pace with the balloon.
Among them were some small
parakeets.

They were especially animated,
swooping around and over them in
splendid formation, like a squadron
of airplanes.

90

Ariel began an earnest conversation with them.

At last he turned to Digby and Percy and said, "My friends, I'm afraid the time has come for me to leave you. I can't possibly go back to live with Lou Ella."

"You would be very welcome to come and live in my house," Digby offered.

But Ariel shook his head politely.

"Thank you, no. I'm afraid it wouldn't do. She would always be close by with her silly chatter; it would be very bad for my nerves. Thanks to your comradeship on this adventure, I have regained my confidence to spread my wings and fly again."

"Where will you go?"

"Well, I've been talking to my good friends here, the parakeets. They have made a home on a delightful island not far from here—*not* a traffic island, I can assure you—one with plenty of fruit and nuts and a stream of clear water, and they have invited me to join them.

"They are keen to improve their language skills, and I think I can help them there. So I have decided to go with them."

"We will miss you!" said Digby.

"I'll keep in touch. The parakeets are very helpful in delivering notes and letters."

It was sad to say good-bye. Digby and Percy watched as Ariel launched himself into the air and joined the great flock of birds, wheeling and calling and making a great clamor in their joy at flying free.

Digby sighed as he watched them disappearing toward a bank of gold-edged clouds.

"It must be jolly nearly supper time!" said Percy.

Luckily the wind continued to blow them in the right direction. When at last they arrived back at the playing fields, Bill the balloon man helped them to land without difficulty.

"You've been out a long time," he said. "I was beginning to get worried about you."

Digby and Percy strolled homeward together.

"What a big adventure!" said Digby. "It's sad that we won't be seeing Ariel next door anymore, but he will be far happier on his island. We might even visit him there one day."

DIGBY O'DAY

"I feel like we've been away for a lot longer than just a day, don't you, Digby?" said Percy. "And I'm SO hungry! Let's stop at the Didsworth Cottage Creamery for tea and cakes before planning what to cook for supper!"

When at last they returned to
Digby's house, they saw Lou Ella
lurking in her front garden. She gave
them a furious look over the hedge.

"Where's Ariel?" she demanded.

"Ariel? Oh, he won't be coming back. He's found a much better place to live and so he's decided to leave you."

"Good riddance!" replied Lou Ella.

"As a matter of fact, I've spoken to the man at the pet shop already. I've decided to get a nice obedient rabbit next."

"If Lou Ella does get a rabbit, I don't envy him," muttered Digby as they opened the front door.

"Perhaps we can help him burrow his way out!"

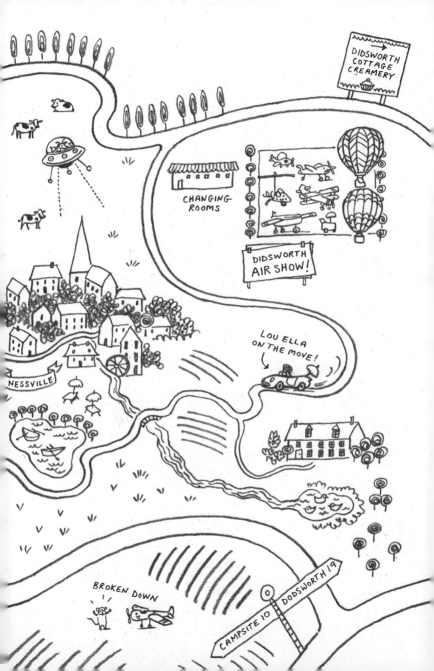

Shirley is Clara's mum, and together they have created Digby and Percy's adventures. Let's find out more about them!

Hello, Shirley and Clara!

Like Digby and Percy, can you tell us something you've always longed to do?

SHIRLEY: *I've always longed to be able to sing (in tune!).*

CLARA: *I wish I could ride in a hot-air balloon, just like Digby and Percy.*

Now, would you prefer to be able to fly or to be invisible, and why?

CLARA: *I would prefer to be invisible so I could get up close to the fiercest animals, like tigers and bears.*

SHIRLEY: *I would prefer to fly, as I do in my dreams.*

If you could fly anywhere, where would you choose?

SHIRLEY: *Somewhere warm and sunny, as long as I could be home by bedtime!*

CLARA: *Me too. We could travel by hot-air balloon—hold on to your hat, Mum!*

Tell us about your pets; do they have any special talents like Ariel?

SHIRLEY: *I have no pets now, but I used to have a tabby cat called Leggy.*

CLARA: *I have a goat called Lucky. He doesn't live in my house, but with lots of other goats in the country. His special talent is that he can spell: if I spell out loud B-R-E-A-K-F-A-S-T, he comes running over!*

And finally, tell us about a time when you were especially brave.

CLARA: *In P.E. lessons when I was young, because I couldn't do any of the sports.*

SHIRLEY: *When, at school, I told the playground bully to get lost.*

Wonderful, Shirley and Clara — thank you for sharing your brave moments with us!

Digby and Percy's Games

Digby and Percy get stuck on a traffic island in the rain—they don't even have a bar of chocolate with them! Here are some games for you to play if you're stuck without a pen and paper or a ball.

The Name Game

Pick a category, like animals or countries. One person goes first and names a country (if that's what you've picked). The next person has to name a country that begins with the last letter of the country named, and so on. Digby and Percy pick pop stars—and Percy always chooses Peaches Meow!

Which Hand?

Choose a small item that fits into the palm of your hand. Put both hands behind your back, then hold the item in one of your closed hands. When you bring your fists to the front, your opponent must guess which hand the item is in.

Telephone

One person whispers a short story—two or three sentences—to the next person, who then has to whisper the same story to the next person. Once the story has been whispered around all the players, the last person says what they have heard. You'll be amazed how different it is from what was originally whispered!

I Went Shopping . . .

One person starts by saying, "I went shopping and I bought a cream cake." The next person says, "I went shopping and I bought a cream cake and a gingerbread man." Each person adds a new item and must remember the items that went before. What kind of silly items can you dream up? When Digby and Percy play, Percy always gets very hungry, because he always chooses delicious things to eat!

Rock, Paper, Scissors

Two people make a fist with one of their hands, then they count to three. On three, both make one of three shapes: Rock (fingers curled in a fist), Paper (fingers flat and touching one another, like a sheet of paper), or Scissors (two fingers sticking out, cutting like scissors). In every combination there is a winner and a loser:

Rock beats Scissors (because it blunts them).

Paper beats Rock (because it wraps around it).

Scissors beat Paper (because they cut it).

There are ten differences between these two pictures— can you spot them all? (Answers on the next page.)

Fabulous Flying Machines

Can you draw your own fabulous flying machine?

How many wings does it have?
What color is it?
Does it fly like a bird,
or soar like a balloon?

How many people will fit
inside your flying machine,
and how high will it go?

The sky's the limit!

When you've come up with your design,
share it with a friend
or hang it on the fridge.

The Digby O'Day Quiz

Digby has written a special quiz to test you! How much can you remember about *Digby O'Day: Up, Up, and Away*?

1. Who repaired Digby's car?

2. Where is the big Air Show held?

3. True or false: Percy is scared of heights.

4. True or false: Digby, Percy, and Lou Ella float away in the hot-air balloon.

5. Where did Ariel used to live?

6. True or false: They land on a traffic island.

7. Do they have any food with them on their adventure?

8. Who was in the Didsworth Forest Folk Fellowship?

9. True or false: Bill the balloon man catches up with the balloon first.

10. Who gets a parking ticket?

11. Who goes to live with the parakeets?

12. Where do Digby and Percy go for tea and cakes?

ANSWERS
1. Don Barrakan 2. The Didsworth playing field 3. False 4. False 5. An island 6. True 7. No 8. Digby and Percy 9. False 10. Lou Ella 11. Ariel 12. The Didsworth Cottage Creamery

If you enjoyed

DIGBY O'DAY

Up, Up, and Away,

then you'll love Digby and Percy's
next adventure,

DIGBY O'DAY

and the
Haunted House

Keep reading for your first chapter. . . .

DiGBY O'DAY
and the Haunted House

Chapter One

Digby was planning a camping trip and he invited his friend Percy to join him.

"What we need is the simple life, Percy!" he said. "We won't go to a campsite with all those cafés and table tennis and showers with running hot water. We'll go somewhere where there are no other people and we can be alone with nature!"

"Sounds great," Percy agreed. But he added, "Nothing wrong with a nice hot shower, though!"

On the morning of their departure, Digby got up very early. After a quick breakfast, he began packing the trunk of his car with a small tent, two sleeping bags and groundsheets, a portable cooking stove, and a few basic provisions.

It was some time before Percy arrived. He was loaded down with all sorts of things, including books, a radio, a Scrabble set, his ukulele, and plenty of chocolate.

"Surely we don't need all that,"

said Digby. "This is supposed to be the simple life, remember?"

But Percy firmly packed them in the car.

Digby's nosy neighbor, Lou Ella, had come to her front gate to watch.

"I hope the weather stays fine for you," she said. "The forecast on the radio said it was going to rain later."

Digby and Percy ignored her. She was still standing there watching them as they drove off.

They drove for several hours with Digby at the wheel. Percy read the road map.

At last they left the motorway

behind and reached some beautiful open countryside. They saw a sign pointing to the Happy Down Campsite, but Digby sped past. As they did so, Percy caught a glimpse of the friendly family, Mum, Dad, and the three little ones, settling down in their comfortable camper van, with hot showers near at hand and a shop in case they needed extra supplies, and he felt a small pang of envy. But Digby kept going, and soon they turned onto a winding lane with high hedges on either side.

They passed only one house,

a very old one, set well back from the lane behind unkempt bushes. Its walls were covered in ivy, and its uncurtained windows looked out blankly from beneath a tumbledown roof.

"I don't much like the look of that place," said Percy. "Doesn't seem like there's anyone living there. A bit spooky, if you ask me."

They kept going until at last Digby stopped the car by a five-barred gate. They both got out and peered over it into the field beyond.

"This looks just right," said

Digby enthusiastically. "I do believe there's a stream down there by those trees. It's an ideal spot!"

Right away he scrambled through a hole in the hedge.

"You begin unpacking the car, Percy," he called back. "I'll pile our things up on this side. Then we'll pick out a really good place to pitch our tent."

Neither of them had noticed the sign near the gate that read:

STRICTLY PRIVATE—KEEP OUT! TRESPASSERS WILL BE PROSECUTED!

and the Haunted House

Digby and Percy's camping trip won't all go as planned. There are terrible calamities and spooky happenings awaiting our daring duo — and things that go bump in the night. . . . Will Digby and Percy find out the truth about the old dark house?

Find out in

DiGBY O'DAY

and the Haunted House